An ARTHUR Reader

ARTHUR
AND THE
SCARE-YOUR-PANTS-OFF
CLUB

Other ARTHUR Readers
by Marc Brown

MARC BROWN

ARTHUR
AND THE
SCARE-YOUR-PANTS-OFF
CLUB

SCARE·YOUR·PANTS·OFF
BOOKS

RED FOX

For Tolon

A Red Fox Book

Published by Random House Children's Books
20 Vauxhall Bridge Road, London SW1V 2SA

A division of The Random House Group Ltd
London Melbourne Sydney Auckland
Johannesburg and agencies throughout the world

Copyright © 1998 Marc Brown

Text by Stephen Kerensky, based on the teleplay by Terence Taylor

First published in the United States of America by Little, Brown & Company, and simultaneously in Canada by Little, Brown & Company (Canada) Limited 1998

Red Fox edition 1999

3 5 7 9 10 8 6 4

Printed and bound in Great Britain by Cox & Wyman Ltd, Reading, Berkshire

Papers used by The Random House Group Limited are natural, recyclable products made from wood grown in sustainable forest. The manufacturing processes conform to the environmental regulations of the country of origin.

THE RANDOM HOUSE GROUP Limited Reg. No. 954009

ISBN 0 09 940313 7

Chapter 1

• • • • • • • • • • •

'I'm hungry,' said D.W.

She was sitting in the kitchen, waiting for breakfast.

'Be patient, sweetie,' said her mother. 'Your father's almost ready.'

D.W. drummed her fingers on the table. She didn't like to be patient. It took too long. And the only thing worse that being patient was being *told* to be patient.

'Just another moment,' said Mr Read. He was busy at the cooker. 'Lightly browned . . . a little icing sugar . . .'

'Yummm,' said D.W. She licked her lips.

'Yummm, yummm,' said baby Kate in her high chair. She licked her lips, too.

'Don't take too long, dear,' said Mrs Read. 'The kids are revving up.'

Mr Read picked up the plate and brought it towards the table. 'Ta-dah!' he announced. 'By special request, my World-Famous Whoopee Waffles. The favourite of presidents, professional athletes, and rock stars. There's whole-grain goodness in every bite.'

'Whoopee!' said D.W.

'Now, if I could just have your plates, I'll be happy to serve —'

Arthur rushed in.

'Morning, Mom, Dad ... Gotta run. Oops!'

Arthur unexpectedly collided with his father, knocking the waffles high into the air.

D.W. gasped.

Arthur pointed.

But Mr Read sprang into action. He caught the falling waffles on the plate, then dished them onto the table.

D.W. clapped. 'My hero!' she said.

Her father took a bow. 'Lucky I spent that summer waiting on tables in the Catskills.'

'More,' said baby Kate.

Mr Read smiled. 'I don't think so, honey. Let's not push my luck.'

'Sorry,' said Arthur. 'I guess I wasn't looking where I was going.'

'I guess not,' his mother agreed. 'But why are you in such a hurry?'

Arthur sat down to eat. 'I have to get to the library.' He stuffed half a waffle into his mouth.

'Slow down a little,' said his mother. 'Drink some juice. You don't want to choke. What's at the library that can't wait for waffles?'

'The new Scare-Your-Pants-Off Club

book will be there today. I want to be first in line.'

Mrs Read was impressed. 'You're going to the library? On a Saturday? Of your own free will?'

'Wow!' said his father. 'Hard to argue with that. But aren't you exaggerating a little? Are these books really flying off the shelves?'

'Just about,' said Arthur. 'They're really popular. I waited three weeks for the last one.'

'Why do you think everyone likes them so much?' asked his mother.

Arthur wasn't sure. 'Maybe it's because they're sort of scary and fun at the same time.'

'An unusual combination,' said Mr Read.

'Right,' said Arthur. He swallowed another bite and dashed for the door.

Then he was gone.

'I don't see what the big deal is,' said D.W. 'But I think it's great that Arthur is going to the library.'

'Why is that?' asked her mother.

D.W. eyed the plate. 'Because,' she said, 'it leaves more waffles for me!'

Chapter 2

Arthur hurried down the street. He was thinking about the new book he would soon be reading. He wondered how he would get the pants scared off him this time. Last month's *Which Witch is Which?* had started him shivering by the third page.

Arthur jumped high over a drain. He didn't want some creature from the Underworld rising through the holes to grab him. It was just that sort of carelessness that had cost Susie so dearly in *Night of the Cornstalker*.

Arthur turned the corner and saw the library ahead of him.

'Oh, no!'

Outside the building, a long line of kids had already formed. It snaked down the steps and along the pavement.

'Hi, Arthur!'

'Over here!'

At the end of the line, Francine, Buster, Sue Ellen, and the Brain were waving to him.

Arthur trudged over to join them. The line was so long! It was unbelievable.

'Guess we should have met earlier,' said Francine.

'Yeah,' said the Brain. 'Like just before dawn.'

'Hey!' said Buster. 'Let's not jump to conclusions. Who knows? Maybe they're just all here to study.'

'On a Saturday?' said Francine.

Sue Ellen yawned. *'Early* on a Saturday?' she added.

Arthur sighed. 'I don't think so, Buster. Besides, everyone I just passed is wearing a SYPOC T-shirt or hat.'

'Even once we get in,' said Francine, 'there won't be any new books left.'

'I guess we could check out some of the old ones to read again,' said Arthur.

Buster nodded. 'Yeah. How about *Curse of the Mummy's Breath*? Talk about not brushing your teeth . . .'

'Or *Skeletons in the Closet*,' said the Brain. 'I wore the same clothes for a week after I read that one.'

The clouds rolled overhead, and the sun disappeared.

'Don't forget the scariest one of all,' said Francine. *'Zombie Substitute Teacher.'*

'Oooooh!' everyone said together.

They all shuddered.

'I wonder why that TV truck is here,' said Buster. He pointed across the street.

'Maybe the reporters are fans, too,' said Sue Ellen.

'Or maybe,' said the Brain, 'it's news to see a line outside a library on a Saturday morning.'

'Never mind that,' said Francine. 'Look! The doors are opening.'

They all turned to watch. The library doors creaked open slowly. A sinister shadow appeared within, slowly moving forwards. The sun came back out as the shadow reached the steps.

'Good morning,' said Ms Turner, the librarian. 'This is quite a turnout.'

The kids cheered.

She held up a hand to hush the crowd.

'It's a pleasure to see you all. However, I have some bad news. Anyone who has come to check out the new Scare-Your-Pants-Off Club book today will be unable

to do so. In fact, all of the books in that series have been removed from our shelves until further notice.'

The kids were stunned. They let out a shriek of disbelief.

'I've been waiting for an hour!'

'Not fair!'

'What happened?'

Ms Turner held a finger to her lips. 'That's all I can say at this time. Naturally you're welcome to come in and pick out something else. But quietly. Remember, this is a library.'

She went back inside.

The doors closed behind her – and nobody rushed to open them again.

Chapter 3

• • • • • • • • • • • •

'I don't get it,' said Arthur as the kids walked away. 'Who would want to get rid of our books?'

'Not all our books,' Francine reminded him. 'Just the Scare-Your-Pants-Off Club books.'

'Why pick on them?' asked Buster.

Nobody had a quick answer.

'Hey!' said Sue Ellen. 'Look at that!'

She pointed to a TV store across the street. The SYPOC logo filled the screen.

Everyone crossed the street to find out what was going on.

'*In suburban Elwood City,*' said the news

17

reporter, '*a parents group has chased some children's books off the shelves of the public library.*'

The picture showed the library and all the kids waiting in line.

'That's us,' said the Brain.

'How did we get on TV so fast?' asked Buster.

'I imagine,' said the Brain, 'that they used a satellite to get these pictures back to the studio.'

'Shhh!' said Francine. 'I want to hear the rest.'

'*The parents group, called PAWS – Parents Against Weird Stories – says the scary stories are bad for kids. We tried unsuccessfully to reach E. A. D'Poe, the author of the books, for comment. Hoping to build more support, PAWS is holding a rally for concerned parents. They will meet on the library steps at one o'clock tomorrow afternoon.*'

The news moved on to other stories.

'Red alert!' Buster shouted. 'If we ever want the pants scared off us again, we've got to do something – and fast.'

'But what?' asked Francine.

The Brain scratched his head. 'Generally speaking,' he said, 'minors have limited access to legal recourse or arbitration.'

'Which means,' said Arthur, 'that there isn't much we can do.' He looked around at his friends. 'But I'm not willing to give up yet. We've never given up before!'

'Sure we have,' said Buster.

'Lots of times,' said Francine.

'We're good at giving up,' said Sue Ellen.

'Not when it's important,' said Arthur. 'Remember the time you helped clean out my garage so I could go with you to see *Galaxy Avengers*?'

Arthur remembered it well.

Francine was carrying two heavy bags of rubbish. The Brain was stacking tins of paint, and Arthur was lining up planks of wood against the wall.

Buster was sweeping the floor. When he finished, he started balancing the broom on his nose. Suddenly the broom fell off, knocking over the planks of wood. They fell onto the tins of paint, which opened and spilled paint everywhere.

Francine was so startled that she dropped the rubbish bags, and all the contents tumbled out.

'I remember that,' said Francine. 'Nice going, Buster!'

'It was an accident!' said Buster. 'It could have happened to anyone.'

'The point is,' said Arthur, 'we made it to the film.'

'The *next* day,' said the Brain. 'After we cleaned up everything.'

'OK,' said Arthur, 'so we hit a few

bumps along the way. What about the time Buster needed help with his maths?'

Buster was sitting on his couch, deep in concentration. His homework and maths books were spread out around him. 'Come on, Buster,' said Arthur. 'You can get this.'

He and Francine were wearing the numbers 7 and 3 on their chests. Pal was standing between them with an x, the multiplication symbol, draped over him. The Brain had an equals sign taped to his forehead.

'Think quickly,' said the Brain. 'My forehead is beginning to itch.'

'Twenty-one!' said Buster. 'The answer was twenty-one. I still remember it.'

'See?' said Arthur.

'I'd forgotten about teaching Buster to multiply,' said Francine. 'If we can do that, maybe we can do this, too.'

'I know,' said Buster. 'Let's go on strike! No more homework till we get our books back.'

Arthur sighed.

The Brain folded his arms.

Francine rolled her eyes.

'All right, all right,' said Buster. 'It was worth a try. But who has a better idea?'

Nobody did – not yet, anyway.

Chapter 4

• • • • • • • • • • •

Just after lunch, Arthur, Buster, Francine, the Brain, and Sue Ellen met at The Sugar Bowl.

'What we need to do,' said the Brain, 'is quantitatively demonstrate that we're not alone in our opinion.'

'Huh?' said Buster.

'He means,' said Francine, 'we have to show PAWS that a lot of kids want their books back.'

'I wonder where Muffy is,' said Francine. 'I called and left a message for her to join us.'

'We can't wait for her,' said Buster.

'We have to move, move, move! We have to take action.'

'I have one idea,' said Francine. 'We could get signatures on a petition. That's what my mom did to save the old City Hall building. If we can show the PAWS people how much support the books have, maybe we can change their minds.'

'But it can't just be kids' support,' said the Brain. 'We'll need adults, too.'

'Do we have enough time?' said Sue Ellen. 'The PAWS rally is tomorrow.'

'Well,' said Arthur, 'there's only one way to find out.'

The kids split into several groups and spread out through the town. Buster and Arthur teamed up on Arthur's front lawn.

'Goooooood morning, Elwood City!' Buster shouted into a loud-hailer.

Two cars whizzed by without stopping.

'Step right up!' Buster went on. 'See the Amazing Arthur perform feats of wonder! Then sign your name to save our books.'

Arthur was wearing a diving mask and swimming trunks. He was trying to balance on a rope above an inflatable paddling pool.

'Buster, are you sure about this?' Arthur asked. He didn't feel very amazing. He didn't think he looked amazing, either.

'It's like an advert,' Buster whispered. 'Before we can get them to sign, we have to get their attention. Now, go ahead!'

Arthur took a breath and started along the rope, balancing himself with a broom.

A few kids passing by stopped to watch.

'Easy, there!'

'Whoa! Back! Back!'

Arthur leaned one way, then the other. As the broom twirled like a propeller, he fell into the water.

The kids laughed. 'Again! Again!' they shouted.

'The Amazing Arthur will be happy to perform again,' said Buster. 'But first a word from our sponsor.'

He pulled out the petition and explained what they were trying to do.

While Arthur dried off with a towel, the kids signed their names.

Meanwhile, Francine and Sue Ellen were jumping double Dutch in the park. A line of kids was waiting for a turn to jump.

Francine was chanting.

'PAWS has taken our books away,
So I'm asking for your help today.
Line up now and sign your name.
That's the point of my rope game.'

As each kid finished, he or she signed the petition.

'Next!' said Francine.

Over at the bus stop, the Brain was trying to educate the waiting passengers. He had covered a blackboard with flow charts, equations, and names of books.

'As you can see,' he told the crowd, 'we predict that the impact on school performance will be geometric. Note the marked rise in the learning curve.'

He pointed with his pointer.

The bus passengers shook their heads. A few covered their ears.

'It is our hypothesis,' the Brain went on, 'that recreational reading yields many educational benefits. Therefore, we invite you to sign our petition.'

'We'll sign,' said someone, 'if you promise to stop explaining things to us.'

'Yes, please!'

'By all means.'

'We agree.'

They crowded around the Brain's clipboard.

He smiled. If everyone else was having the same success he was, they might have a chance after all.

Chapter 5

●●●●●●●●●●●

After Arthur and Buster had collected all the signatures they could in the neighbourhood, they went to the park to gather more.

'Are you sure you don't want to be the Amazing Arthur here, too?' Buster asked.

Arthur was sure. He had been amazing enough for one day.

'Let's split up,' he said. 'That way we can cover more ground.'

Buster headed for the seating area around the pond while Arthur set out across the fields.

At first Arthur had trouble catching up

with people who were rollerblading or cycling or just playing games.

'Sorry, we're busy.'

'Catch me later.'

'Not now. We're at match point.'

It was a little discouraging. He did spot an old woman tending some plants near a fountain. Finally, someone who wasn't on the move.

He walked over to introduce himself.

'Excuse me, ma'am,' he said. 'Could I speak to you for a moment?'

'You already are,' said the woman. Her glasses were perched low on her nose. 'It's a little late to ask my permission.'

Arthur hesitated. 'I guess that's true. It's for a good cause, though. At least, we think it is.'

'And what is this good cause, may I ask?'

'A parents group has had our favourite

books removed from the library,' Arthur explained. 'We're trying to get them back. But we want to show that a lot of people feel the same way we do. So we've started up this petition. Would you sign it for us?'

The woman paused. 'I see I'm not the only one doing volunteer work today.' She gave Arthur a long look. 'It all depends on the books. I wouldn't want to go against your parents wishes.'

'Oh, you wouldn't be. My parents like me to read different things. My father says it's like the food groups. It's healthy to have a little bit of everything.'

'Good advice,' said the woman.

'Besides,' said Arthur, 'these books are our favourites: the Scare-Your-Pants-Off Club books.'

The old woman sat back on her heels and pushed her glasses back up on her nose.

'Really? The Scare-Your-Pants-Off Club books? Do you read them . . . um . . .?'

'Arthur.' He shook her hand. 'Do I read them? Of course! I haven't missed a single one.'

The woman frowned. 'Then the situation *is* serious. Maybe I should speak to this parents group myself!'

She stood up and gathered her gardening tools.

'Don't give up, Arthur. You and your friends are doing a good thing.'

Arthur looked puzzled. 'Sure. Thanks – I think . . .'

He watched her leave. Then he looked down at his clipboard. 'Hey! Wait! You forgot to sign.'

But the woman was gone.

Chapter 6

• • • • • • • • • • •

Later that afternoon, Arthur, Francine, Sue Ellen and Buster walked out of The Sugar Bowl, eating ice cream cones.

'Collecting signatures is hard work,' said Buster.

'Do you think we have enough names?' asked Francine.

Arthur licked the drips around his cone. 'I think so. There are pages and pages. I just hope PAWS will listen to us.'

Francine looked at her watch. 'I wondered where the Brain is. He was supposed to meet us at five.'

'Look!' said Buster. 'Here comes Muffy.'

'Where has she been, anyway?' said Francine. 'We could have used her help today.'

Muffy was wearing a big smile. 'Great news, everyone!' she announced. 'My parents are having a big party tomorrow at WonderWorld.' She paused. 'And I can invite anyone I want.'

'Wow!' said Arthur. WonderWorld was the best carnival and theme part around. Going there for free would be a real treat.

'That's terrific,' said Sue Ellen.

'Count me in!' said Francine.

Francine noticed Muffy eyeing her cone.

'Want a lick?' she asked. She held out the cone.

Muffy backed away. 'Um, no thanks. My mom won't let me – too much fat and sugar.' She shut her eyes. 'Take it away. Please!'

At that moment the Brain came around the corner. He was clutching a newspaper in one hand.

'Sorry I'm late, everyone. Wait till you hear what I just —' He stopped suddenly. 'Oh . . . hello, Muffy.'

Muffy looked at the pavement.

'What did you find out?' Francine asked.

The Brain glanced in Muffy's direction.

'Listen to this,' he said. 'There's a whole article in today's paper about the book ban and an interview with the people behind it. I'll skip to the important part.'

He started reading from the newspaper.

'"*Kids don't know the harm these books do,*" *said Millicent Crosswire.* "*My poor daughter, Muffy, read just one, and it gave her awful nightmares.*"'

Everyone looked at Muffy. She continued to study the cracks in the pavement.

The Brain read some more. '"*We started PAWS to save other kids," added Millicent's husband, Ed. "We're having a big rally for concerned parents at the library tomorrow. Afterwards, all our supporters – young and old – can join us for a celebration at WonderWorld."*'

Buster was shocked. 'Muffy, your mom and dad started PAWS?'

Muffy looked up. 'Yes,' she said.

'But why?' asked Francine.

Muffy bit her lip.

'Let me see that,' Arthur said to the Brain.

The Brain gave him the newspaper.

Arthur read through the interview. 'This isn't just any old WonderWorld party,' he said. 'Is it, Muffy? It's only for people who support PAWS.'

Muffy shrugged. 'Well, if you want to get technical . . .'

'Oh, no!' said Buster.

'We have to get our books back, Muffy,' said Arthur. 'Don't you understand?'

Muffy hesitated. Then she took a deep breath and folded her arms.

'You just have to decide which means more to you,' she said. 'WonderWorld – or a bunch of silly books. The choice is yours.'

Chapter 7

• • • • • • • • • • •

'I don't know what's so complicated,' said D.W. She put out her hands as though she were balancing things in a scale. 'Some creepy books here. Free WonderWorld here.' She lowered her WonderWorld hand to her knees, as though it was holding something heavy. The other hand shot up. 'No contest.'

She and Arthur were sitting in the living room. Arthur had told her about the problem with Muffy and her parents.

'It's not that simple,' said Arthur.

D.W. laughed. 'It is to me. You know how great WonderWorld is. They have the best roller coaster. People throw up and everything. What do you think, Kate?'

Their baby sister was watching from her playpen. Her hands were going up and down.

'See, Arthur?' said D.W. 'Even Kate knows the right thing to do. And she's just a baby.'

'The right thing to do about what?' asked Mrs Read, taking a break from her work.

'Arthur gets to go to WonderWorld for free,' said D.W.

'Really?' said Mrs Read. 'How did that come about?'

Arthur told her.

'I see,' said his mother. 'Well, Arthur, for someone going to WonderWorld, you don't look very happy.'

Arthur sighed. 'As I was trying to tell D.W., it's not that simple. I don't want to miss Muffy's party. But I don't want to lose my favourite books, either. And it's not really right to go if I don't support PAWS.'

Mrs Read nodded. 'It's a difficult situation, Arthur. It's like a balance sheet. There are pluses and minuses. When you add everything up, you have to do what you think is right – even if it means making a sacrifice.'

Arthur wandered outside to think some more. Why did sticking up for what you believe in have to be so difficult?

'I wish I knew what everyone else was thinking,' Arthur muttered.

'I'll tell you what I'm thinking,' said his father from the garage. 'My life's an open book. A cookbook, that is.' Mr Read was busy with a huge catering job. But right now, he was looking through boxes.

'I wish there was a book where I could

44

look up the answers to hard questions,' Arthur said.

He explained the situation to his father.

'That would be a good book to have,' his father agreed. 'Probably a best seller.' He opened a box. 'Ah, here's what I was looking for.'

He pulled out a clown costume. 'Just what I need for this afternoon's children's hospital benefit.'

He began putting the costume on.

'What if I'm the only one who decides to protest against PAWS?' said Arthur. 'What if all my friends decide to go to WonderWorld instead?'

Mr Read adjusted his bald wig. 'Can't be afraid to look foolish for something you believe in. Pass me that rubber nose, please.'

Arthur handed it to him. Then he sat down to think.

Bllaaattttt!

Arthur jumped up.

'Oh, thanks,' said his father. 'I wondered where that whoopee cushion was.' Mr Read put it in his pocket.

He looked at his watch.

'I've got to be going. Remember one thing, Arthur. I know you want to do what your friends are doing. But look at me.'

Arthur stared at his father in his clown suit.

'Sometimes clowns work as a team.' His father shook hands with a bunch of imaginary clowns around him. 'And sometimes they stand under the spotlight all by themselves.' He made a little bow.

Arthur sighed. And sometimes clowns looked sad, the way he felt right now.

Chapter 8

• • • • • • • • • • •

At the library the next morning, the Cross-wires stood at the top of the steps. Muffy kept ducking behind her parents, but they kept pulling her out in front of them.

A crowd of kids and parents was gathering around them.

Mr Crosswire spoke into a portable microphone. 'Thank you all for coming. I'm Ed Crosswire of Crosswire Motors, corner of Park and Lakewood, open most nights till ten. But I'm not doing this for me. I'm doing it to save our kids!'

His words were met by cheers and polite applause.

Off to the side, Arthur stood with his mother. He was holding up a sign that said, KEEP YOUR PAWS OFF OUR BOOKS!

Nobody seemed to be paying attention.

'I don't see anyone,' said Arthur. 'I guess WonderWorld wins.'

'Don't be too sure,' said Mrs Read. 'There's still time.'

'This is our little girl,' Ed Crosswire continued. He held up Muffy's hand. 'We started PAWS because of her, but we care about all of you as well.'

At that moment Buster, Francine, the Brain, and Sue Ellen came around the corner. They were holding signs over their heads.

OBEY THE LAWS – NOT PAWS!

CLOSE THE BOOK ON PAWS!

'You're here!' said Arthur. 'I was beginning to wonder.'

'Sorry we're late,' said the Brain. 'We stopped for more signatures.'

He held out the petition sheets. There were now dozens and dozens of names.

'So who's going to give these to Mr Crosswire?' Buster asked.

'You do it,' said the Brain.

'Not me,' said Buster. 'You do it.'

'Who?' said Sue Ellen.

'Not you,' said Francine. 'How about Arthur?'

'Yeah!'

'Good idea.'

'Well, Arthur . . .' said the Brain.

Arthur took a deep breath. 'All right,' he said. 'I'll do it.'

Holding the petitions under one arm, he worked his way through the crowd.

No Ferris wheel. No ice cream. No roller coaster.

'Excuse me. Excuse me. Coming through.'

No candyfloss. No bumper cars. No haunted house.

At the top of the steps, Arthur stopped in front of Mr Crosswire. He would be sorry to miss all those great things at WonderWorld. But this was more important.

'If we don't make a stand now, we will have failed in our trust. We must —'

'Excuse me, please, Mr Crosswire,' said Arthur. 'We need to talk.'

'Not now, Arthur. I'm on a roll.'

'That's just it, Mr Crosswire. You're rolling right over our rights. It's not fair. Speaking for the kids, we really want our books back. We've got these signatures of support —'

'That's nice, Arthur. I admire your spirit. But believe me, this is for your own good! These books are trouble with a capital *T*.'

'Have you read them?' asked a voice from the crowd.

Arthur turned around. That voice was familiar.

Surprisingly, it was familiar to Ed Crosswire, too. He looked out over the crowd. He seemed a little confused.

Arthur wondered what would happen next.

Chapter 9

●●●●●●●●●●

'Who is that?' asked Ed Crosswire.

The rest of the crowd was silent.

'Answer the question,' said the voice. 'Have you read the books you're condemning?'

The crowd pulled back to reveal the speaker. Arthur recognized her. She was the woman he had spoken with in the park.

Mr Crosswire cleared his throat. 'I am proud to say that I wouldn't read these books if you paid me!'

The woman sighed. 'I'm not surprised,' she said.

Mr Crosswire looked startled. 'Why, I

know you . . . You're Miss McWord, my school English teacher.'

'Yes, I am, Edward.' She walked up the steps. 'I'm glad to see your memory hasn't failed you – even if your common sense has.'

'Miss McWord, I assure you I have every bit as much common sense as I ever did.'

She stood beside him. 'That may be true,' she admitted. 'I see you haven't changed. You never were much of a reader. Can you appreciate how hard a writer works to create stories kids will like to read? Each story is like a seed, Edward. If a child reads one, the seed may grow into the desire to read another. That's something every writer hopes for.'

Mr Crosswire crossed his arms. 'Oh, really? Miss McWord, you were certainly a fine teacher. But what makes you such an expert about what writers hope for?'

'Well, I'm a writer myself.'

'Oh. I'm sure we're all delighted to hear that.' Mr Crosswire hesitated. 'Anything we know?'

Miss McWord straightened Mr Crosswire's jacket and flicked some lint from his shoulder. 'Nothing you've read, Edward, considering your common sense and all. But since you've asked, I'm the author of the Scare-Your-Pants-Off Club books.'

'You!' said Mr Crosswire, turning pale. He had a sudden vision of Miss McWord walking him down to the head teacher's office.

'You?' said Arthur.

'Her?' Francine, Buster, Sue Ellen, and the Brain said together.

The woman nodded. 'E. A. D'Poe is my pen name.'

Muffy nearly exploded with excitement. 'Ms D'Poe!' she cried. 'I'm your number-one fan! I have all your books. Could I have your —' Her parents glared at her. 'Ooooops!' She clasped her hand across her mouth as her parents surrounded her.

'You read them all?' said her father.

'And just when did you do that?' asked her mother. 'Mary Alice Crosswire, you've got some fancy explaining to do.'

'Uh-oh!' said Muffy.

'If you've read all of these books,' said Mrs Crosswire, 'then obviously it wasn't one of them that gave you the nightmare. What was it?'

'Um, well . . .' Muffy hated it when her mother sounded like a detective.

'Just a minute, here,' said Mr Crosswire. He stared at Muffy. 'Now I know who ate my tub of Haasen-Pfeffer ice cream.'

'And was then afraid to admit it,' said her mother. 'Mary Alice, you know eating like that gives you bad dreams.'

'We're very disappointed in you,' said her father.

'And I'm disappointed in you, too,' Muffy's mother said to her husband. 'What were you doing with a tub of that ice cream, anyway?'

'Well, I . . .'

Arthur almost smiled. Muffy and her father were both standing with their hands hanging low. They looked very much alike.

Miss McWord cleared her throat. 'I hate to interrupt a promising family squabble, but we've still got some business to settle. Edward, maybe you can take your foot out of your mouth long enough to listen to one of my stories. That way you can make an informed decision about who should be reading them.'

'Oh. Yes. Excellent idea.'

At this particular moment, anything was better than facing his wife.

Chapter 10

• • • • • • • • • • • •

'And since that night, nobody has dared to steal anything from the haunted hamburger stand again.'

Miss McWord put down her book.

The crowd clapped and cheered. Among the loudest fans was Ed Crosswire.

'Well, Daddy?' Muffy asked.

He sighed. 'I guess I shouldn't have tried to stop you kids from reading books without knowing *the whole story* myself.'

'Maybe,' said Miss McWord, 'you have changed after all, Edward.'

'So can we have our books back, Mr Crosswire?' Arthur asked.

'I will disband PAWS on one condition,' said Mr Crosswire.

Everyone fell silent.

'And that condition is?' said Muffy.

'That Miss McWord will read us another story.' Mr Crosswire looked at her. 'Please?'

'Yes!'

'Another one!'

'All right!'

Miss McWord smiled, something she didn't do very often. She opened another book.

'*No one in the village knew why the old man lived all alone, deep in the dark woods. Only the animals of the forest knew his secret . . .*'

Arthur sat back and closed his eyes as a familiar chill crept up his spine.